W9-CGU-070

Ants in My Pants

Written by Norma Vantrease
Illustrated by Steve Cox

SCHOLASTIC INC.

New York   Toronto   London   Auckland   Sydney
Mexico City   New Delhi   Hong Kong   Buenos Aires

This book is dedicated to Richard and Ryan, my biggest fans.
—N.V.

To my children, Genevieve and Joe
—S.C.

Reading Consultants

Linda Cornwell
Literacy Specialist

Katharine A. Kane
Education Consultant
(Retired, San Diego County Office of Education and San Diego State University)

ISBN 0-516-24818-9

12 11 10 9 8 7 6 5 4 3   7 8 9/0

Printed in China.   62

First Scholastic book club printing, November 2004

Ants come in the window.
They crawl right down the wall.

3

They run across the carpet.
They tiptoe in the hall.

They are looking for the kitchen.
They want jam or maybe bread.

I see them in a circle.

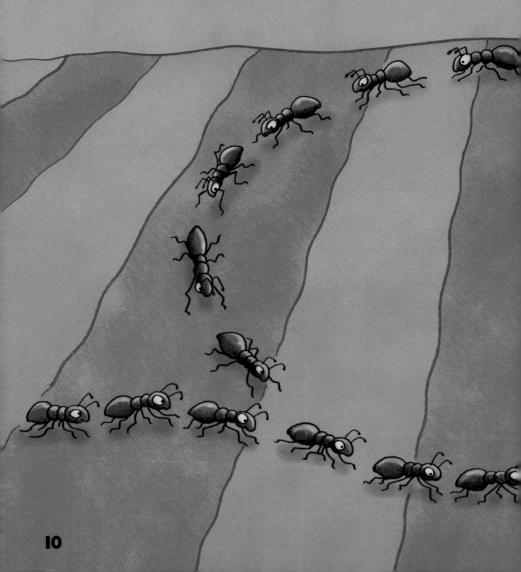

There are *twenty*, maybe more.

First they talk together.
Then they march across the floor.

They crawl inside my closet.
They find my favorite pants.

Over. Under. In and out.
My pants are full of ants.

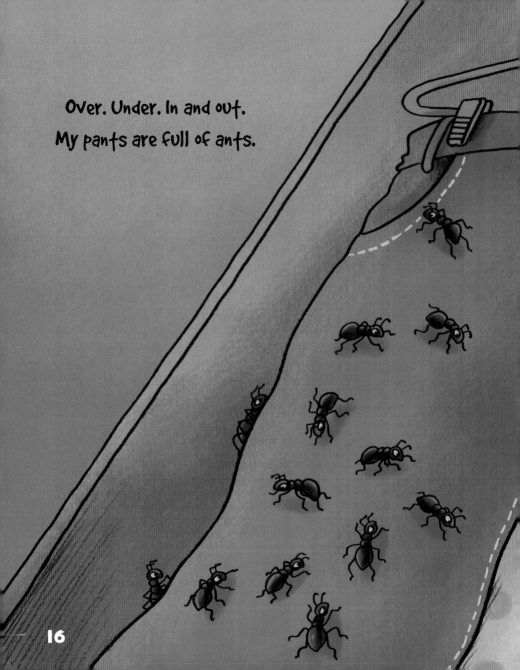

There are crumbs inside the pocket.
There is jelly on the knee.

19

They chew and chew.
They chomp and chomp.
There is nothing left for me.

They are full and tired.
I see them fall asleep.

Tiptoe. Tiptoe. Here I come.
I never make a peep.

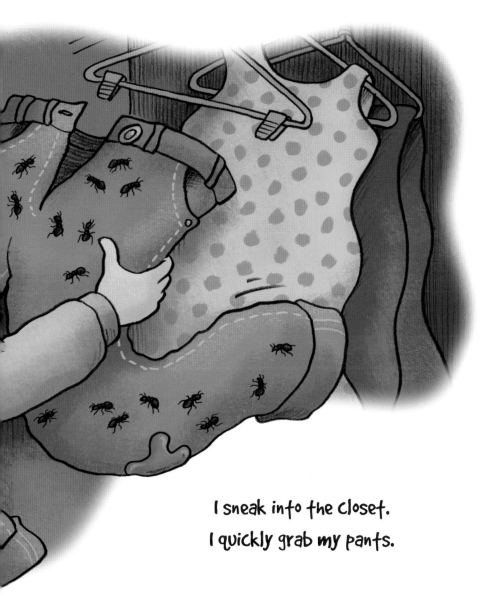

I sneak into the closet.
I quickly grab my pants.

I run outside. I shake, shake, shake.

I rid my pants of ants.

Word List (79 words)

a	crumbs	into	of	sneak
across	down	is	on	talk
and	fall	jam	or	the
ants	favorite	jelly	out	them
are	find	kitchen	outside	then
around	first	knee	over	there
asleep	floor	left	pants	they
bedroom	for	looking	peek	tiptoe
bread	full	make	peep	tired
carpet	grab	march	pocket	together
chew	hall	maybe	quickly	twenty
chomp	here	me	rid	under
circle	I	more	right	wall
closet	in	my	run	want
come	inside	never	see	window
crawl	instead	nothing	shake	

About the Author

Although *Ants in My Pants* is Norma Vantrease's first book with Children's Press, she has been creating children's stories for many years, first as a teacher and now as an author. Her work has appeared in children's magazines. When she is not writing and illustrating, Norma is a children's art instructor. She lives in central Florida with her husband, Richard, and their cat, Minnie.

About the Illustrator

Steve Cox lives and works in the city of Bristol, England. He has always enjoyed drawing and making up characters since childhood, so now he feels lucky to be able to do it almost every day for a living. He enjoys creating images that complement a story line, while injecting a little bit of humor of his own wherever possible.